Published by Advance Publishers, L.C.
Maitland, FL 32751 USA
www.advancepublishers.com
Produced by Judy O Productions, Inc.
Designed by SunDried Penguin

Printed in the United States of America


First published 2004.

In the land of Agrabah, there lived a poor beggar boy named Aladdin. He lived there with his best friend, a pet monkey, named Abu. Aladdin dreamed that someday he'd be rich and live in a palace.

Inside the palace of Agrabah, the Sultan was trying to find a husband for his daughter, Princess Jasmine. But Jasmine didn't want to get married unless it was for love. Poor Jasmine felt trapped – she'd never even been outside the palace walls – and her only friend was Rajar the tiger.

The Sultan trusted his advisor Jafar and spoke to him about Jasmine. But the evil Jafar was only interested in power. He was desperate to get the magic lamp which was hidden inside the Cave of Wonders and the only person permitted to enter the cave was a "Diamond in the Rough" (one whose worth lay far within). Jafar asked the Sands of Time to reveal such a person, and it was ... Aladdin! Jafar sent his guards to capture him.

Meanwhile, in the palace Jasmine decided to run away. The next morning, as she walked through the marketplace, Aladdin saw her get into trouble with one of the storeowners. Aladdin came to her rescue but then Jafar's guards arrived to capture him. Jasmine revealed herself as the princess to save Aladdin but the guards said their orders came from Jafar and they dragged him away. When Jasmine raced back to the palace to beg Jafar to let Aladdin go, he told her Aladdin was already dead.

But Aladdin wasn't dead, he was being held prisoner in the palace dungeon. Just as his monkey, Abu, was helping him escape, Jafar, disguised as an old man, came to Aladdin and told him about the Cave of Wonders. He asked Aladdin to help him get the magic lamp and in return Aladdin would be rich, and sure to impress Princess Jasmine. Aladdin agreed and went with the old man to the cave.

Inside the cave, Aladdin was guided by a magic carpet to find the lamp, but just as he got it, Abu grabbed a large jewel and the cave began to collapse. As they tried to escape, Jafar grabbed at the lamp and pushed Aladdin and Abu back into the cave. But Abu managed to steal the lamp back before they were trapped inside.

When Aladdin rubbed the lamp, a Genie appeared! Aladdin was his new master, the Genie said, and he would grant Aladdin three wishes, then he helped them escape. After promising his last wish would be to set the Genie free, Aladdin made his first wish – to be a prince so that Princess Jasmine would want to marry him.

At the palace, Jafar was still angry at the loss of the lamp and was trying to convince the Sultan to let *him* marry Princess Jasmine. But when Aladdin arrived in the disguise of Prince Ali Ababwa, the Sultan thought he would be the perfect husband for his daughter – Jasmine was angry. "How dare you! I'm not a prize to be won!" she shouted. That night, though, Aladdin took her for a ride on the magic carpet and she began to fall in love with him, not realizing he was really Aladdin.

Later, however, Jafar's guards captured Aladdin again and threw him into the sea. The Genie rescued him, using Aladdin's second wish, and they returned to the palace just in time to stop Jafar from hypnotizing the Sultan into letting him marry Jasmine. Jasmine and Aladdin were married.

Meanwhile, Jafar's parrot, Iago, stole the lamp from Aladdin's room and Jafar became the Genie's master. His first wish was to become the Sultan of Agrabah and the Genie had to grant the wish. Then Jafar wished to be a powerful sorcerer. The Genie granted his wish and Jafar changed Aladdin back into a beggar, before sending him far away. But, luckily, the magic carpet appeared and helped Aladdin get back to the palace again.

In the palace, Aladdin found Jafar and tricked him. He told Jafar that the Genie was much more powerful than Jafar would ever be. Jafar got really angry and wished to become a Genie. The Genie granted his final wish but Jafar forgot that a Genie is a prisoner of his lamp – and he disappeared into a black, glowing lamp, trapped forever.

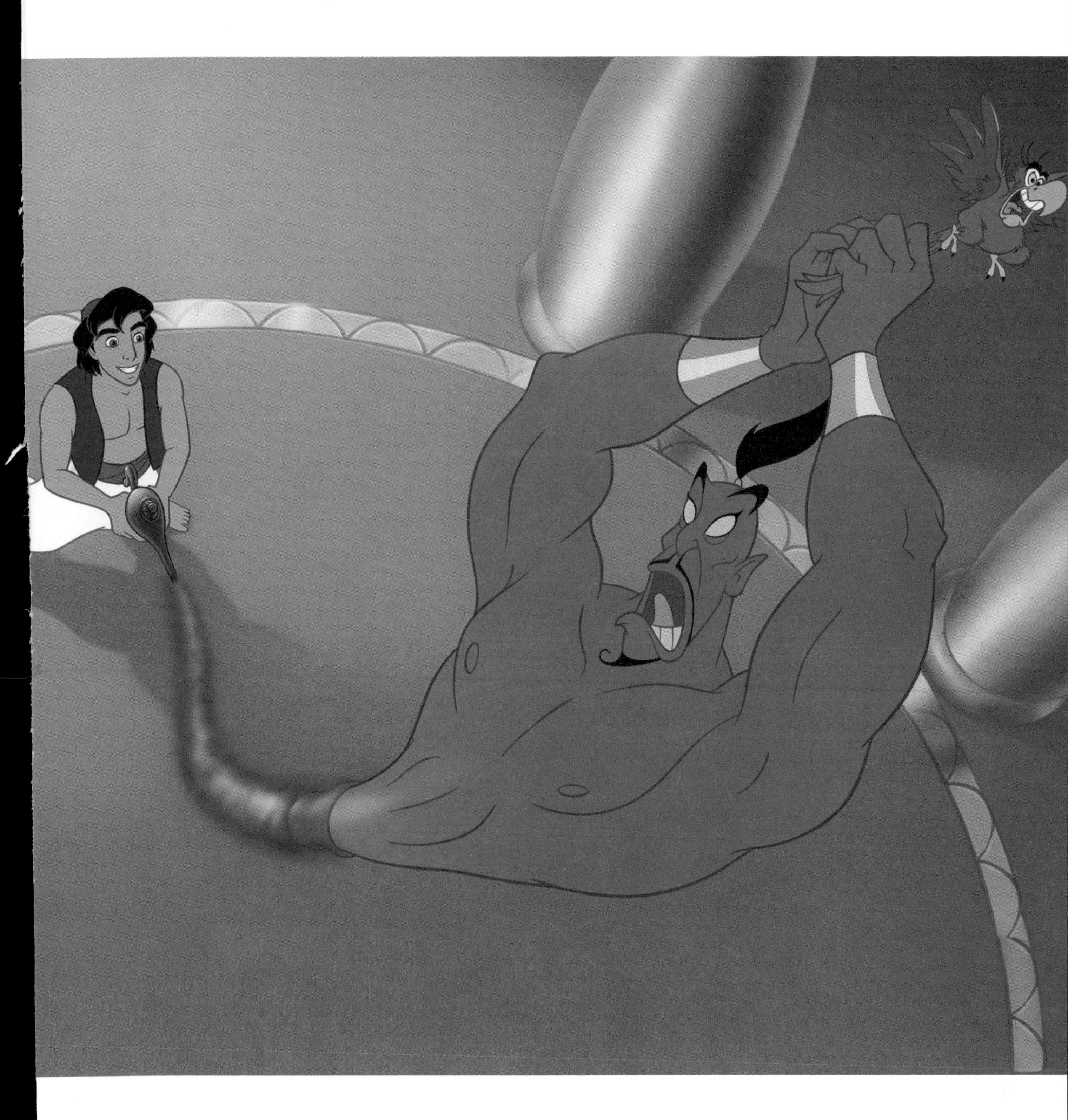

With Jafar gone, Aladdin was again the master of the Genie. He kept his promise and made his last wish to free the Genie. Then Jasmine and Aladdin flew off together on the magic carpet to discover a whole new world.

*The End*